Praise for my other books

KT-221-323

'Will make you laugh out loud, cringe and snigger, all at the same time'
—LoveReading4Kids

'Very funny and cheeky'
—Booktictac, Guardian Online Review

Waterstones Children's Book Prize Shortlistee!

'I LAUGHED SO MUCH, I THOUGHT THAT I WAS GOING TO BURST!'
Finbar, aged 9

'The review of the eight year old boy in our house...
"Can I keep it to give to a friend?"
Best recommendation you can get' —Observer

'HUGELY ENJOYABLE, SURREAL CHAOS'
—Guardian

I am still not a Loser
WINNER of
The Roald Dahl
FUNNY PRIZE
2013

EGMONT

We bring stories to life

First published in Great Britain 2014
by Egmont UK Ltd
The Yellow Building, 1 Nicholas Road, London W11 4AN

Text and illustration copyright © Jim Smith 2014
The moral rights of the author-illustrator have been asserted.

ISBN 978 1 4052 6801 1

barryloser.com
www.egmont.co.uk

A CIP catalogue record for this title is available from the British Library

Printed and bound in Great Britain by the CPI Group

69033/001

All rights reserved. No part of this publication may be reproduced,
stored in a retrieval system, or transmitted, in any form or by any means,
electronic, mechanical, photocopying, recording or otherwise, without the prior
permission of the publisher and copyright owner.

Stay safe online. Any website addresses listed in this book are correct at the time
of going to print. However, Egmont is not responsible for content hosted by third
parties. Please be aware that online content can be subject to change and websites
can contain content that is unsuitable for children. We advise that all children are
supervised when using the internet.

Egmont takes its responsibility to the planet and its inhabitants very seriously.
We aim to use papers from well-managed forests run by responsible suppliers.

sort of
I am↑a
Loser

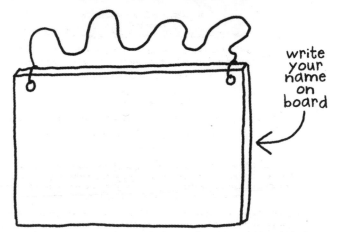

write
your
name
on
board

Barry Loser

Pages numbered by Jim Smith

Super-loser

I've always wanted to be a superhero like my favourite TV star, **Future Ratboy**. That's why I've started calling myself . . . Superloser!

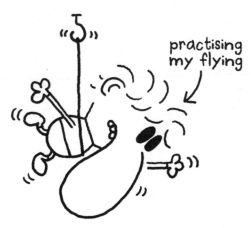

"ک"

practising my flying

Superloser's catchphrase is 'keel!', which is what **Future Ratboy** says instead of 'cool'.

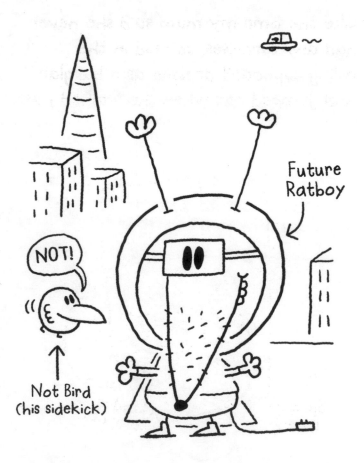

Future Ratboy

NOT!

Not Bird
(his sidekick)

My superpower is loserkeelness, which is where I'm always coming up with brilliant and amazing ideas.

Like the time my mum said she never had any surprises, so I hid in the airing cupboard dressed as a burglar and jumped out when she walked past.

AARRGGHH!!

Burglar Barry

my mum (landed in compost)

Loserkeelness is also where you accidentally tread in a dog poo, or turn the wart on your thumb into a remote control for yourself or something like that, and all your friends laugh and think you're really loserkeel.

forwards/
backwards

wart

pretending
I'm a robot

Everyone at school knows I'm the loserkeelest person ever.

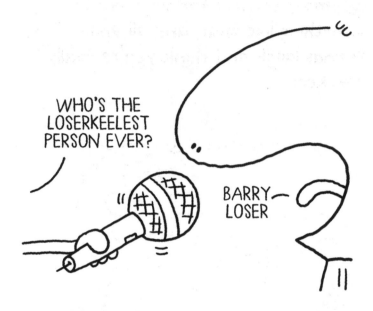

WHO'S THE LOSERKEELEST PERSON EVER?

BARRY LOSER

So imagine how annoying it was when Fay Snoggles came in one day acting even more loserkeel than me . . .

Fay Snoggles

'What's that white plastic board thingy hanging round your neck?' said Sharonella, as Fay walked through the classroom door with a white plastic board hanging round her neck.

Sharonella

Fay pulled a big red marker pen out of her pocket and plopped the lid off.

'GOT SORE THROAT,' she wrote on the board. 'HURT TO SPEAK.'

this is Fay in case you didn't know

She wiped the board clean with a tissue and blew her nose like an elephant, leaving a red pen-smudge on the end of her nose, and everyone laughed, apart from me.

totally unfunny

'Oh my days, Fay, you are making me LARF!' snorted Sharonella, who's been fake best friends with Fay ever since her real best friends Donnatella and Tracy fell out with her for copying the way they draw dogs.

'Isn't this the sort of loserish thing YOU'D do, Barry?' burped Darren Darrenofski, swinging Fay's board round and almost slicing the red bit off her nose.

Darren

still not funny

He flumped over his desk and poked me in the earhole with his fat little finger.

'Yeah, except I'd do it a million times more loserkeely,' I said, pretending I wasn't bothered.

I looked out the window at all the wind that was blowing, not that you can actually SEE wind, even if you're a superloser like me.

what wind
looks like

A poster saying 'YOU COULD BE CLASS CAPTAIN!' blew across the playground, and I remembered our teacher Miss Spivak saying the elections for Class Captain were coming up.

that poster
I was just
talking about

'What you gonna do, Barry? Fay's COM-PER-LEET-ER-LY copying your loserkeelness!' said Bunky, who's sort of like my sidekick.

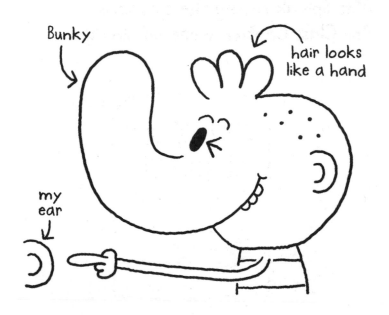

Bunky

hair looks like a hand

my ear

He poked his finger into my OTHER earhole, and I bonked him on the nose for being such a naughty best friendypoos.

Because of all the fingers in my ears
I couldn't really hear anything, apart
from what I was thinking.

'Bunky's right, Superloser. Fay's
completely copying your loserkeelness!'
said the voice inside my head, and
I imagined it coming out of a tiny little
mini Barry, sitting on my brain like it
was a sofa.

real
Barry

mini
Barry

'Yeah, Superloser, you've got to come up with one of your brilliant and amazekeel ideas!' said another mini Barry, and I nodded my head, imagining the mini Barrys falling off their brain sofa because of all the nodding I was doing.

mini Barry

(don't really have a spring neck)

me nodding

'Listening to your mini Barrys, are you?' said Nancy Verkenwerken's voice all of a sudden.

I was just about to tell her to get out of my head, when I realised she'd pulled Darren and Bunky's fingers out of my earholes and was speaking into my actual ear with her real-life mouth.

Nancy

my
ear
hole

'Looks like you've got some competition, doesn't it?' she smiled, pointing over at Fay, who was blowing her nose again, this time like a warthog.

That's the annoying thing about Nancy, she can always tell what I'm thinking.

'Oh yeah, like I'm really bothered!'
I said, leaning back in my chair just
enough to fall over. 'ARRRGGGHHH!' I
screamed, waggling my arms around
like the loserkeelest superloser ever.

← totally
loserkeel

But nobody noticed, because they
were all too busy laughing at Fay.

Verbunkenloser Whatever Boxes

Verbunkenloser Ltd is me, Bunky and Nancy's new company. It only sells one thing at the moment, but in the future it's gonna be bigger than Feeko's Supermarkets.

'Roll up, roll up, get your
Verbunkenloser Whatever Boxes
here! Only a few left!' shouted Nancy
from behind the table-tennis table
in the playground, which is where
we set up our pyramid of Whatever
Boxes every lunchtime.

When I first came up with the idea
of selling old cereal boxes filled with
whatever rubbish we had lying around,
I wasn't sure anyone would buy them.
But it's turned out to be a big hit,
mainly thank* to Nancy.

*only one thank, though

'Ooh, me! Me!' squeaked Jocelyn Twiggs, handing Nancy the dirtiest, bent-in-halfest coin ever and taking a box off the top of the pyramid.

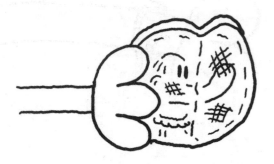

It was a Feeko's cereal packet painted light blue, with the word 'Whatever' scribbled on it in black felt-tip pen.

He ripped the lid off, stuck his hand inside and pulled out a worm. 'A real-life worm! Just what I've always wanted!' he grinned.

'And it doubles up nicely as a bracelet,' said Nancy, curling it round Jocelyn's wrist.

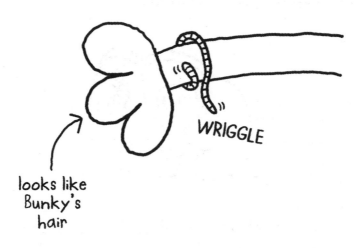

looks like Bunky's hair

WRIGGLE

Jocelyn did a face like he didn't know what was more funny, having a worm curled round your wrist or wearing a bracelet. Then he shrugged and bounced off, and I wondered if the worm was thinking it was all a bit funny too.

Gordon Smugly glided over and picked up a box, and the pyramid swayed.

always horrible to me

'Hmmm . . . good weight, interesting rattle . . . I'll take it,' he said, putting a coin into my hand, and I popped it into the plastic Feeko's ice cream tub, which is where we keep all our money.

FEEKO'S
ICE CREAM

'Is that the one?' whispered Bunky,
and I snortle-nodded, even though
I wasn't really in a snortle-nodding
sort of mood what with Fay
COM-PER-LEET-ER-LY copying
my loserkeelness and everything.

Gordon slid his finger along the top of
the box and opened the flap. 'Raisins!'
he smiled, grabbing a handful of tiny,
brownish, dried-up, bobbly balls and
opening his disgusting mouth.

'Yeah, my NOSTRIL raisins!' Bunky laughed.

'EUUURRGGGHHHYYUCK!' screamed Gordon, throwing the bogies into the air, and they swirled off in the wind like tiny planets. 'Ha ha, nice one Bunky,' he said, not wanting to look stupid, and he walked away with his box of bogie raisins still rattling.

not coming soon

Nancy turned round and gave us one of her looks. 'If we're going to make a success of Verbunkenloser Ltd, we cannot afford to annoy our customers,' she said, tidying up the pyramid.

SWISH

Another poster saying 'YOU COULD BE CLASS CAPTAIN!' blew in front of my eyes like a magician's cape. Sharonella and Fay appeared from behind it and I did a little blowoff out of shock and annoyedness.

'WHA-EH-VA,' said Sharonella, reading the box she'd picked up. 'What's inside? Not that I'm bothered . . .'

'You never know with a Verbunkenloser Whatever Box!' smiled Nancy like she was on TV. 'But every one's a winner!'

'Ooh, random! Go on Fay, you can't lose!' said Sharonella, nudging Fay forwards, and I looked at the pyramid of Whatever Boxes swaying in the wind and came up with one of my brilliant and amazekeel ideas right there and then on the spot.

me coming up with
one of my ideas

Fay pulled her pen out and plopped the lid off. 'ONE PLEASE,' she wrote, sliding a coin towards Bunky and picking up a box. She opened the lid and peered inside.

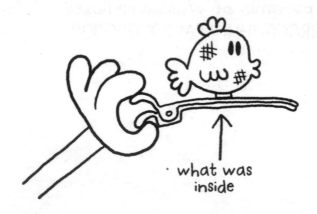

what was
inside

'Ru-ub-bish!' moaned Sharonella, as Fay's hand pulled out a smelly old hair clip with a faded plastic goldfish perched on it that I'd found down a drain.

I stepped forwards and got ready
to play it loserkeel.

'Woohoo! Fay is a winner, everyone!'
I shouted, pretending to trip on a
piece of gravel and fall towards
the pyramid of Whatever Boxes.
'ARRRGGGHHHH! I'M SOOOOOOO
LOSERKEEEELLLL!!!' I screamed,
crashing into them.

Light-blue boxes flew into the air like rectangle chunks of sky and my nose thudded on to the floor, me following behind it.

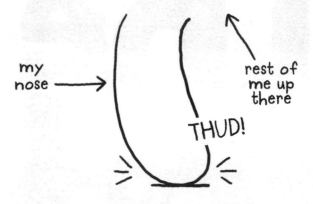

my nose →

rest of me up there

THUD!

'That is SO you, Barry!' laughed Sharonella as I lay on the ground covered in Whatever Boxes, and I breathed a sigh of relief, because I was back to being the loserkeelest person in my class.

The end

(Not really.)

Mogden Poo

It felt good being the most loserkeel person in my class again, and to celebrate I'd come up with ANOTHER one of my brilliant and amazekeel ideas.

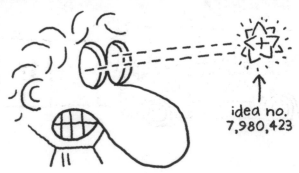

idea no.
7,980,423

It was the next day and we were in the school coach on the way to Mogden Poo.

Mogden Poo is our town's swimming pool, except the 'L' from the sign disappeared one night eight million years ago and no one ever found it.

trunks wrapped
in towel like a
sandwich

'Don't forget, aim them right for my
nose!' I whispered into Bunky's ear as
we jumped out of the coach and ran
into the changing rooms, Darren
Darrenofski blowing off with
excitement behind us.

One of the keel things about the changing rooms at Mogden Poo is that the girls' and boys' are right next to each other with a wall in-between that doesn't go all the way up to the ceiling, so you can spy on the girls getting changed.

← fly doing backstroke

'I can see Donnatella's pants!' screamed Stuart Shmendrix, wobbling on top of Darren and peering over the wall.

'ARRGGGHHH!' shrieked the girls from their changing room, and I looked over at Bunky and gave him the signal.

I was on the spying-wall side of the room, doing my **Future Ratboy** super-high-speed pants-into-swimming-trunks change, and Bunky was by the door.

trunks

pants

I counted down from five in my head and got ready to look like the most loserkeel superloser ever.

The most loserkeel superloser ever

The elastic strap on Bunky's swimming goggles twanged as they shot out of his hands towards my face.

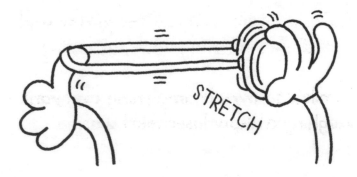

STRETCH

As they flew across the room, I went through the plan in my head:

1. Get hit in the nose by Bunky's goggles

2. Start spinning around, screaming like a loser

3. Tangle myself up in the towel hanging on the hook next to me

4. Stumble into the showers like a blind ghost

5. Accidentally turn on the water and end up lying in a puddle, groaning

I smiled to myself, imagining everyone laughing at how loserkeel I was.

Then I realised I'd managed to do the whole list inside my head AND a smile to myself, all with the goggles still not hitting my nose.

I looked up and saw them shooting over the wall into the girls' changing rooms.

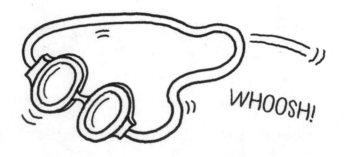

WHOOSH!

'FAY BABES!!! WATCH OUT!' screamed Sharonella, then everything went quiet.

I climbed up Darren Darrenofski, then Stuart Shmendrix, and peered over the wall.

Fay was lying in a puddle in the
showers, tangled up in a towel like
a blind ghost, groaning, with all the girls
laughing at how loserkeel she looked.

'It's exactly like you planned it,
except it all happened to Fay instead!'
whispered a mini Barry in my brain,
and I tried to swivel my eyeballs all the
way round and give him one of
my looks.

bogies
also
angry

'Get your OWN loserkeelness!' I shouted, falling off Darren and Stuart and accidentally landing in the towel bin, which normally would've been really funny and loserkeel, except everyone was too busy laughing at Fay.

FLUMPFH!

Nobody likes a show-off

'Work it, ladies!' boomed an old wrinkled-up man in shiny shorts as I walked out to the swimming pool. His voice echoed off the water and bounced around the ginormous glass windows.

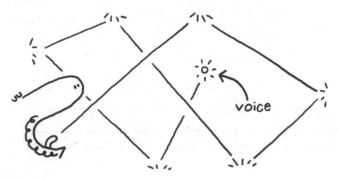

voice

He was dancing along the side of the pool, kicking his legs out and clapping his hands. The whole of his head was completely bald apart from a little grey beard that went all the way round his mouth, like a hairy donut.

CLAP!

I looked into the water and saw Granny Harumpadunk and her friends Ethel, Doreen and Three Thumb Rita from the sweet shop splashing about like they were being attacked by granny-eating sharks.

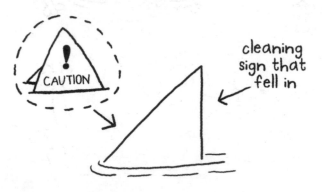

cleaning sign that fell in

'What in the keelness are THEY doing here?' whispered a mini Barry inside my brain, then I saw a sign that said 'AQUA AEROBICS FOR THE ELDERLY' and I nodded my head, imagining the mini Barrys falling off their brain sofa again.

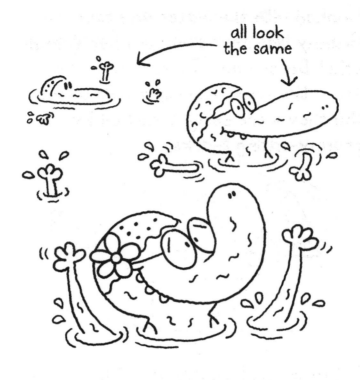

all look
the same

'Cooweee, Barrr-rrrry!' warbled my
granny, waggling her arms at me, and
I was just about to pretend I didn't
know who she was when I had one of
my brilliant and amazekeel ideas.

I glanced along the pool at everyone about to start their lesson and took a deep breath.

'Gwannnnnny!' I shouted, running up to the edge of the water and doing the most loserkeel jump ever. 'Yaaaaayyyyy!' I screamed, landing with a massive splosh.

LEAP!

I opened my eyes underwater and saw Doreen's bum waggling in my face.

that fly from before

'GRANNY BUMS!' I shouted as my head bobbed out of the water and floated there like a duck. I was in-between Doreen and Ethel, who were panting and marching on the spot in super-slow underwater-granny motion.

'Go on girls, burn those biscuits off!' boomed the old man with the hairy donut beard, and I joined in with the grannies, looking over to see if anyone was watching my loserkeelness.

And that was when I spotted Fay limping out of the changing rooms wearing the whiteboard, with an inflatable ring round her waist. She was shivering from the shower and her hair was all over her face.

'Blimey, Snoggles, what happened to you?' chuckled Mr Koops, walking behind her copying her limp, and everyone laughed, some of the old grannies in my aqua aerobics class included.

hasn't
seen him

56

'That's not funny, THIS is!' I shouted, splashing about, giggling and blowing off because of how hilarious and loserkeel I looked.

Mr Koops walked up the side of the pool and stopped next to Donut Beard. I carried on stomping my feet in slow motion and waggling my arms in the air like Ethel.

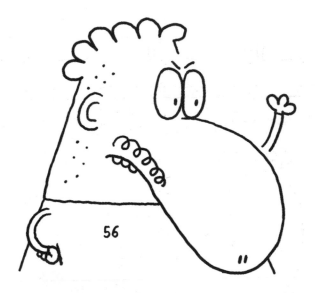

56

'Nobody likes a show-off, Barry,' said Mr Koops all quietly, not even smiling, and I slowed my slow-motion marching down until it completely stopped.

Old granny legs

Mr Koops made me sit at the side of the pool after that, so I found a seat and plonked my bum down on it, then looked to my right and did a massive blowoff out of shock.

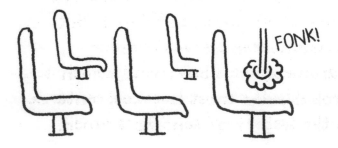

FONK!

Sitting next to me was Mr Hodgepodge, who used to be my teacher at school until he retired because he's about three hundred years old.

The Hodge

'What in the loserkeelness are YOU doing at Mogden Poo?' I said, then I remembered he was Granny Harumpadunk's boyfriend, which is probably the most loserkeel sentence in the history of sentences amen.

'Just waiting to give your old gran a lift home,' he said. 'I see nothing's changed with you, Barry!' he chuckled, giving me a nudge, and I remembered all the times he'd told me off at school.

'It's Fay Snoggles,' I said, pointing over at the pool. She was floating around in her inflatable ring, trying to catch the plastic goldfish hair clip, which had swum off like an actual fish. 'She's completely copying my loserkeelness.'

looks like
Bunky's hair,
and also →
a hand

'Hmmm . . . I thought you DIDN'T want to be a loser?' Mr Hodgepodge said, looking all confused, and I got my mini Barrys to roll my eyes for me from inside my head.

'Loserkeelness is COM-PER-LEET-ER-LY different from being a loser,' I said, poking an old plaster on the floor with my big toe.

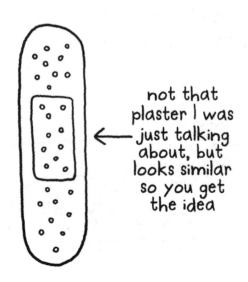

not that plaster I was just talking about, but looks similar so you get the idea

'Yes, well, isn't there an election for Class Captain coming up?' he smiled, nudging me again and waggling his eyebrows, and I remembered those posters that kept blowing past in the wind. 'Maybe you should put yourself forward? There's nothing more loserish than being Class Captain, after all!'

'It's loserKEEL, not loserISH,' I grunted, waggling my foot because the plaster had got stuck.

loserish
brain

loserkeel
brain

'Cor, look at those legs!' whispered
one of the other old ladies' husbands,
tapping Hodge on the shoulder and
nodding over at the grannies, who
were doing underwater handstands
now, waggling their feet in the air.

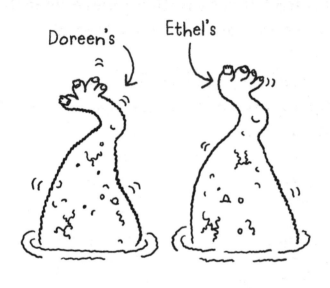

Doreen's   Ethel's

'Ha ha, yes, very nice!' mumbled Hodge,
all embarrassed because of me, not
that I cared.

I swivelled my eyes over to Mr Koops's lesson, mostly to get them away from all the old granny legs, but also to see what was happening. Nancy was synchronized swimming with Jocelyn, and Bunky was floating face down in the water pretending he'd drowned.

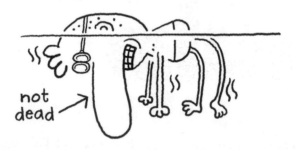

not
dead →

'Barry! Five minutes left. Come and do a dive,' shouted Mr Koops, and I zoomed off from Mr Hodgepodge before he could say anything else about me being Class Captain, because there was no way THAT was ever going to happen amen.

Mini Barry gulp

'Whatever you do, don't blow off!' giggled Darren Darrenofski, clambering up the ladder behind me to the middle diving board. I'd only ever done a dive off the lowest board before, and as I wobbled to the end and peered down I heard one of my mini Barrys do a gulp.

'The people look like ants from here,'
I said, copying what people say when
they're high up. Then I zoomed my
eyes in and realised what I was looking
at was ACTUAL ants, swarming round
that old plaster I was talking about
earlier.

'Come on, Barold!' shouted Darren, and
I reached my arm back and bonked
him on the nose, because I hate it when
people call me that.

I millimetred my toes forwards and took a deep breath.

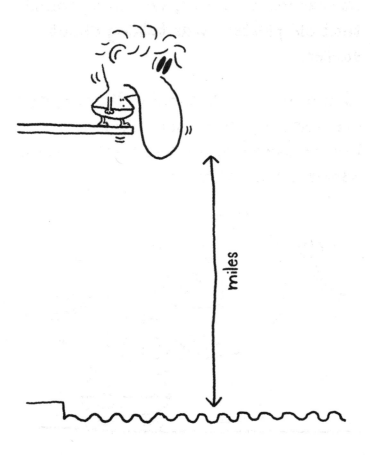

miles

'Go on, Loser!' shouted Mr Hodgepodge from his seat, and the word 'Loser!' echoed off the water and bounced around the ginormous glass windows.

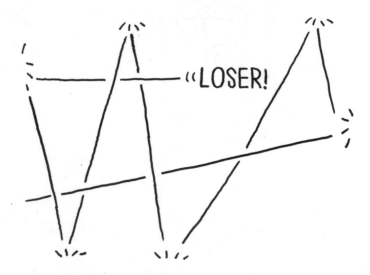

'Loser! Loser! Loser!' chanted my whole class, and some of the old grannies too, so I smiled, even though I'm not a loser, I'm the loserkeelest Superloser ever. And that was when I fell forwards.

'Waaaaahhhhhhhh!' I screamed,
zooming towards the water nose first.

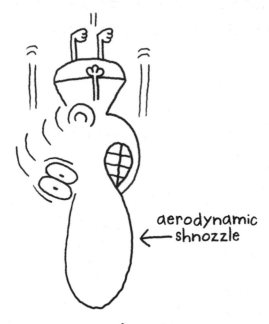

aerodynamic
← shnozzle

You know when you're flying through
the air like **Future Ratboy**, with
everyone chanting 'Loser!' at you,
and you spot Fay Snoggles floating
right next to where you're about to
land? That's what was happening to me.

'OH. MY. DAYS!!!' screamed Sharonella as I did an enormous splosh and a massive wave headed towards Fay. She held on to her white plastic board and started surfing towards the old grannies.

FOOOSH!

'RUN FOR YOUR LIVES, LADIES!' screamed Donut Beard, and the old grannies started old-granny-sprinting away from Fay in super-slow motion.

'THIS IS THE END!' wailed Doreen as she disappeared under the wave, legs and arms and swimming-caps-with-flowers-on-them flying all around.

It took a few minutes for the water to go flat again and for Doreen to surface on the other side of the pool, her false teeth floating next to her.

← Doreen over there

Fay had been swept all the way into the baby pool, which is about a millimetre deep. She was lying in it and rolling from side to side, her inflatable ring doing a super-slow, extra-loud blowoff as it deflaterised.

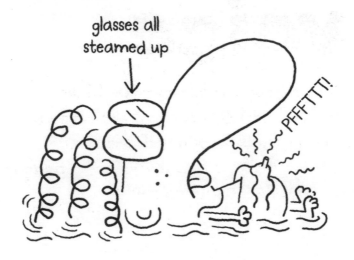

glasses all steamed up

PFFFTTTT!

'That is SO you, Fay!' laughed Sharonella as I climbed out of the water, back to being the second most loserkeel person in my class again.

Future Ratboy voice

'Maybe you SHOULD run for Class Captain,' smiled Nancy as we walked through the school gates the next morning, talking about Mr Hodgepodge and what he'd said to me at Mogden Poo.

'Yeah Barry, there's nothing more loserkeel than being Class Captain!' said Bunky, doing his Class Captain face, and I collapsed to the floor like a pyramid of Whatever Boxes being knocked over, weeing myself with laughter.

full nose waggle

~FFFT!

Jocelyn ran up to us and stopped suddenly, his eyes as wide as Doreen's bum. I looked at his wrist for the worm bracelet from his Whatever Box, but it must've wriggled off because it wasn't there.

now playing: 'Do the Bogie Boogie'

'GRUBBAGE IS COMING!!!' he screamed into my face, then zigzagged off like a poster in the wind.

Grubbage is this loserkeel person who goes round schools dressed up as a bin monster, teaching kids about recycling and saving the planet, and today he was coming to our school.

'Yesss! Grubbage!' whooped Bunky, punching the air and waggling his bum, and I imagined myself as Class Captain showing Grubbage round the school.

punching the air →

POW!

'Fay! Long time no see!' shouted Sharonella, running past us, and I turned round and saw Fay Snoggles bouncing through the front gates WITHOUT her loserkeel whiteboard hanging round her neck.

I don't know if it was being friends with Sharonella, or all the loserkeel attention she'd been COM-PER-LEET-ER-LY stealing off me, but something had changed about Fay. It was like she was turning into a superloser.

'Good mornkeels, Sharonella,' said
Fay, and my ears nearly fell off.
Her voice was still croaky from
having a sore throat, plus it'd gone
a bit squeaky too.

'That voice . . . It sounds familiar,'
murmured Nancy, and I felt my
knees go weak.

'Bunky, hold me, I'm about to fall . . .'
I gurgled, and my vision went blurry
like that time when I was underwater
in front of Doreen's bum.

'Oh my days, Fay! That is, like, the best **Future Ratboy** impression ever!' giggled Sharonella as my legs gave way, and I collapsed to the floor like a pyramid of Whatever Boxes that had only just been stacked back up.

me all collapsed into bits

Planet Dog Poo

'Come along now, kiddywinkles!' shouted Miss Spivak as we walked into the classroom, me still a bit wobbly from my fall. 'As you all know, we have a very special guest today!'

Honk the class parrot was sitting on Miss Spivak's shoulder as per usual, and I wondered if parrots worried about things like being the loserkeelest parrot in their class.

Honk

pencil sharpener

'VERY SPECIAL GUEST!' squawked Honk, sounding exactly like Miss Spivak, and I snortled, even though I wasn't really in a snortling sort of mood.

'Play it keel, loseroids!' I whispered to myself in my best **Future Ratboy** voice, but it was nowhere near as loserkeel as Fay's. Once everyone heard hers, she'd go straight to being the number one loserkeelest person in the whole UNIVERSE.

I looked up at the big green board at the front of the classroom, where Miss Spivak had stuck all the recycling pictures we'd been doing that week.

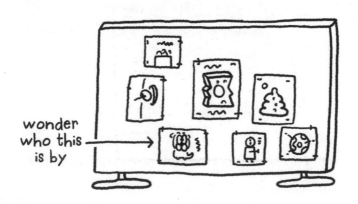

wonder who this is by

Anton Mildew's painting of a crumpled-up cereal box was in the middle, with the words 'PLEEEAASSSEE REECCYYCCLLE' written round it in blue capitals.

Next to that was my amazekeel felt-tip drawing of the earth in the future if we carry on making so much rubbish.

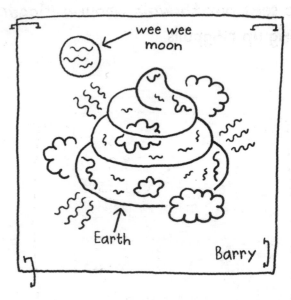

It was based on the episode of **Future Ratboy** when he goes to the Planet Dog Poo, where it's completely impossible not to step in a pile of dog poo at least once every one step.

At the bottom of the board was Fay's drawing of a machine that recycled Fronkle cans into little robots that were sent out to walk around Mogden, picking up ringpulls.

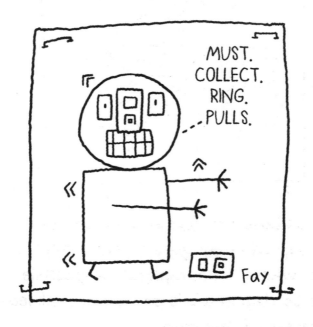

'That's exackerly the sort of loserkeel thing YOU'D come up with!' whispered a mini Barry in my head.

'And she does the best **Future Ratboy** impression ever!' said another one, and I stuck my finger in my earhole and gave it a waggle to shut him up.

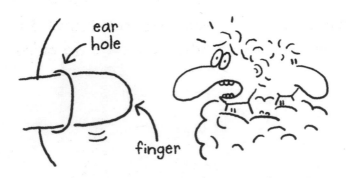

ear hole

finger

'You've got to STOP HER, Superloser!' they shouted all together, and I was just about to nod them off their brain sofa when something behind the big green board started to growl.

'Poo, what's that bin smell?' shouted Gaspar Pink right in my earhole, and I turned round and saw his whole entire face go white.

His eyes were staring past me and he looked as if he was standing on the end of a really high diving board, peering down at the water. 'G-G-G-G-Grubbage!' he whisper-screamed, and I heard both of my mini Barrys do gulps.

((TREMBLE

Grubbage

Standing at the front of the classroom was the most bin-smelling, pile-of-old-socks-looking thing I've ever pointed my eyes and nose at.

'I'MMM GGGRRRUBBAGE!' growled a voice from somewhere inside it, and everybody gasped. 'And I've come here today to talk to you about RRRRUBBIIISH!' Grubbage boomed, shaking himself like a dog, and bottle tops and ringpulls and screwed-up bits of paper fell out of his costume.

'He's got trainers on!' shouted Darren Darrenofski, pointing his chewed-up pencil at Grubbage's feet, and I spotted a pair of Feeko's trainers underneath Grubbage's raggedy trouser legs.

'YOU, BOYYY!' roared Grubbage,
pointing at Darren.

'Me?' said Darren, pointing at himself
with his chewed-up pencil.

'Come HEEERE!' boomed the voice, and
Darren got up and walked to the front
all Darrenishly.

Darren
walking
all
Darrenishly

I glanced out of the window and saw ANOTHER one of those posters saying 'YOU COULD BE CLASS CAPTAIN!' fly past, and I had one of the most brilliant and amazekeel ideas I've ever had in the history of me being alive in this world amen.

'What's your favourite fizzy drink, boyyy?' whisper-growled Grubbage, which is the easiest question to answer in the whole universe, because everyone knows Darren loves Fronkle more than his own mum.

can of Fronkle

Mrs Darrenofski

'FRONKLE!' shouted the whole class, except me, because I was too busy getting ready to tell everyone my plan.

'Fronkle, ehhh? That comes in CANS, doesn't it?' said Grubbage, and one of his costume ears fell off. 'And what do you do with those cans once they're finished?' he asked, as I started to stand up.

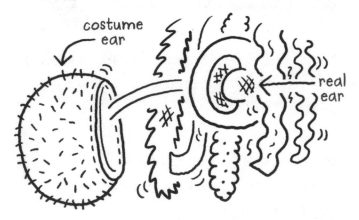

costume ear

real ear

'RECYCLE THEM!' screamed the whole class, and I opened my mouth in slow motion and started to speak.

Captain Barry

'Ladies and gentlekeels,' I said, which is how **Future Ratboy** starts off all his speeches.

'Barry, what in the name of ...' shouted Miss Spivak, but I put my hand up to stop her.

'My apologies, Madam Spivak, but this simply cannot wait,' I said, sounding all Gordon-Smuglyish, and Bunky snortled. 'It is with great loserkeelness that I, Barry Superloser, the most loserkeel person in the history of loserkeelness, officially put my name forward for the job of Class Captain,' I said, in my most **Future Ratboyish** voice ever.

'He's gone completely stark raving bonkers!' laughed Anton Mildew, and Gaspar Pink took a photo, probably for their unkeel newspaper, The Daily Poo.

comes
with
this
stuck
on it

'I'm dreadfully sorry about this,
Grubbage,' said Miss Spivak, running
over to him and slipping on a
chewed-up pencil.

SLIP

Honk flew off her shoulder and on
to Grubbage's head. 'ARRGGGHHHH!
Get this thing off of me!' screamed
Grubbage, bottle tops and ringpulls
flying out of his costume.

'GRUBBAGE! GRUBBAGE!' squawked Honk, pecking at Grubbage's real-life ear, which was sticking out of the hole where his costume one had fallen off.

I looked over at Nancy, who was covering her eyes, then at Bunky, and he gave me a quadruple-reverse-twizzle salute.

I tried to think what sort of things would make people vote for me. Then I remembered how much Darren likes Fronkle . . .

'If elected Class Captain, I would make it the law that we had Fronkle coming out of our taps instead of water,' I said, feeling my loserkeelness getting stronger.

'YESSS!' shouted Darren, dancing around Grubbage, who was flailing his arms about, screaming. Miss Spivak was lying on the floor, scrabbling around for her glasses.

they should make glasses that can talk

Then I looked at Stuart Shmendrix,
who was chewing on a Thumb Sweet,
which are these keel sweets that
Three Thumb Rita sells in her sweet
shop. 'ALSO, all rubbers on the ends
of pencils will be replaced with Thumb
Sweets!' I carried on, making it up on
the spot.

Thumb Sweet   pencil rubber

'Woop!' wooped Stuart, and a bit of
Thumb Sweet flew out of his mouth
and landed on Tracy Pilchard's arm,
next to one of her eight million
bracelets.

I pointed my mouth towards Tracy and opened it, waiting for the words to come out.

'Instead of Maths, there will be a new class all about bracelets and necklaces and stuff like that,' I said, and Tracy stopped doing a drawing of a dog and high fived Donnatella, and I saw Sharonella look a bit sad.

JANGLE

'SOMEBODY GET THIS BIRD OFF ME!'
shouted Grubbage. I felt sorry for him,
but I couldn't stop. I HAD to become
Class Captain before everyone heard
Fay's **Future Ratboy** impression and she
became the loserkeelest person in the
whole universe.

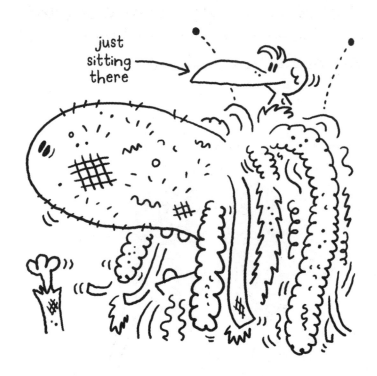

just
sitting
there

'Thank you for listening to me this morning, ladies and gentlekeels, and remember: a vote for Barry is a vote for loserkeelness!' I shouted, and I shut my eyes and smiled.

Which meant I didn't see Fay Snoggles standing up and walking over to Grubbage.

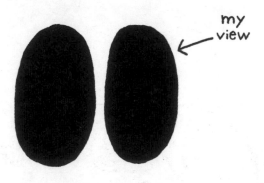

my view

Captain Snoggles

'Here, Honkypoos, here, birdy!' said Fay's voice, sounding exactly like **Future Ratboy** when he talks to his sidekick, Not Bird, and I stopped smiling and opened my eyes.

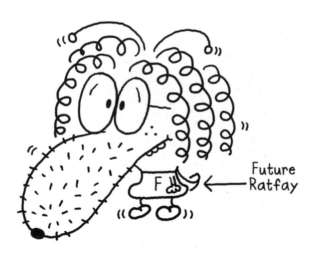

Future
Ratfay

She'd turned her head round and was showing Honk the plastic goldfish hair clip in her hair.

Honk stopped pecking at Grubbage's ear and blinked.

'What is it, Honk, do you like Fay's goldfish?' whispered Miss Spivak, trying to stop him from eating Grubbage's ear. 'Yes, it's shiny, isn't it!' she said, even though it isn't shiny at all, it's completely faded from living down a drain its whole life.

Honk jumped off Grubbage's head and flew over to Fay, landing on her shoulder.

'What a nightmare,' said a voice from inside Grubbage's costume, and he ran out of the classroom leaving a trail of bin smell behind him.

'I am SO sorry, Grubbage,' Miss Spivak called out as the door slammed, then she turned to me. 'What has got into you, Barry?' she shouted.

I looked out at the wind and saw Grubbage wobbling over to his car, yogurt pots and scrumpled-up orange juice cartons flying out of his costume, and felt bad for ruining his day. But at least I was going to be Class Captain.

'I'm sorr-rry, Miss Spi-vaak,' I said, and Gaspar Pink started to take another photo, so I turned towards him and did my loserkeelest smile.

The camera flashed as Sharonella wobbled over to Fay. 'Well I know who I'll be voting for,' she snortled, stroking Honk's head. 'Captain Snoggles!'

feet look like trotters →

'CAPTAIN SNOGGLES!' squawked Honk, pecking at the plastic goldfish in Fay's hair, and I did a blowoff out of COM-PER-LEET annoyance. Not that you could tell, what with all the bin smell in the air.

spot the blowoff

Having a wee

It was after school and I was in my toilet at home, having a wee. Bunky and Nancy were in my kitchen working out how I could beat Fay in the Class Captain elections, because now it was between me and her.

'What if he straps a can of Fronkle on to each foot, so he's taller. Everyone always votes for tall people!' said Bunky, who thinks he's SO keel, just because he's tall.

I tried to wee faster, so I could get back in the kitchen and bonk him on the nose for having such a rubbish idea.

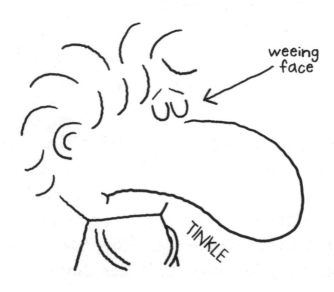

weeing face

TINKLE

Nancy was busy painting Feeko's cereal boxes light blue and writing 'Whatever' on them in felt-tip, not that I could tell because I was in the toilet, like I just said.

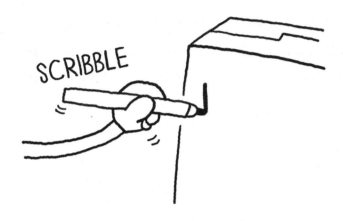

SCRIBBLE

'Don't you think people vote for the person they reckon will do the BEST JOB as Class Captain?' she said, loud enough for me to hear. 'Maybe you need to take it all a bit more seriously, talk about recycling and stuff like that?'

I made a face to myself as I finished my wee, then waggled my fingers under the tap for three milliseconds and made another face, this time to my ACTUAL face, which was in the mirror on the wall above the sink.

'Ooh, Nancy, you are a clever girl,' said my mum, who was also in the kitchen by the way.

'Oh why don't you just swap me for Nancy if that's what you want!' I boomed, appearing at the kitchen door, holding my arms out all Class-Captainly.

Barry & Nancy action figures

my mum choosing Nancy

'Don't be silly, Snookyflumps,' said my mum, but I just ignored her and started pacing up and down the kitchen, trying to come up with one of my brilliant and amazekeel ideas.

'Forget all that "being serious" unloserkeelness, we need to give people what they WANT!' I said, thinking about Darren and his Fronkle-on-tap, and Stuart with his Thumb-Sweet pencil-rubbers. 'What is there that EVERYBODY likes?' I asked.

I darted my eyes around the kitchen, looking at all my mum's knick-knacks, and they landed on the cereal box Nancy was painting.

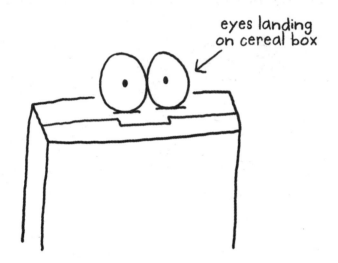

eyes landing on cereal box

'That's IT!' I shouted, doing a jump like Future Ratboy at the end of one of his episodes, and I hit my head on the kitchen light like a COM-PER-LEET and utter superloser.

Barry Boxes

'WHAT'S it?' snortled Bunky, and my mum ran over and gave my head a hug, which I squirmed out of straight away, even though she was holding on really tightly.

'Well, you know how much everyone loves Whatever Boxes?' I said, pointing at the one Nancy was painting.

'Ye-ah?' they all yeahed, splitting their yeahs into two bits, my mum included.

'How about we turn them into BARRY BOXES? Except, instead of selling them, we GIVE THEM AWAY!'

TA-DA!

'Give them away? What's the point of that?' said my mum, flicking on the kettle, and I wondered if she had any friends of her own she could go and play with.

CLICK

'The point, Motheringtons, is that we only give someone a Barry Box if they promise to vote for me in the election!' I said, doing my two-for-the-price-of-one Class-Captain grin-and-wink, waiting to hear the applause.

'Nice plan, Barold, but we only have three Whatever Boxes left,' said Nancy, finishing one off and putting it next to the other two on the kitchen table.

I scratched my bum, trying to think where I could get more cardboard boxes. 'Mu-um, can I have some more cereal boxes, pwease?' I said in my Baby Barry voice, and Nancy pretended to be sick all over Bunky.

BLEURGH!

'You've used them all already, Snookyflumps,' said my mum, opening the cereal cupboard, and a trillion loose cornflakes poured out all over her feet.

You know how I'd just hit my head on the kitchen light? I was still standing underneath it, and the bulb flickered like in a cartoon when someone comes up with an amazing idea.

'What about the money we made from selling Whatever Boxes ... we could buy more boxes with that!' I screamed, and I was just about to run upstairs and grab the plastic ice cream tub full of coins from under my bed when Nancy opened her mouth.

cuddly Future Ratboy

Not Bird duvet

←— ice cream tub

'No, you can't use that! I ... I was saving up for a new, erm ...' Nancy did her face she does when she's trying to make something up.

She grabbed my mum's shopping catalogue that's always lying open on the kitchen table and pointed at a photo of a sun lounger. 'I was saving up for a new sun lounger!' she said, holding up the catalogue.

'Oookaaayyy,' I said, which is how **Future Ratboy** says 'OK' when he doesn't believe someone but can't be bothered to find out what's going on.

I thought of the ice cream tub full of coins, and how I could maybe just borrow a few of them for a couple of days. 'Don't worry, I'll come up with something,' I said, and I hoped Nancy couldn't tell what I was thinking.

mind reader Nancy →

crystal ball →

Mr Feeko's Beard Flakes

It was still dark as I snuck out of my house and skateboarded to Feeko's Supermarket the next morning.

I patted my pocket, hearing the coins jangle, and thought about the empty ice cream tub under my bed.

'You're only BORROWING the money!'
whispered a mini Barry in my head as
I skateboarded into Feeko's and went
straight to the cereal aisle, looking for
the cheapest boxes I could find.

'They're all so expensive!' moaned
another mini Barry, and I felt like my
dad, who's always going on about how
much stuff is.

At the end of the aisle was a massive sign with 'SOMEBODY PLEASE BUY THESE' written on it in big red capitals.

Underneath the sign was a pyramid of 'Mr Feeko's Beard Flakes' boxes.

I Superloser-zoomed my eyes in and saw a cardboard cut-out of Mr Feeko, the billionaire owner of Feeko's Supermarkets, standing next to all the boxes.

He was holding a bowl of Beard Flakes and smiling out from a beard that went all the way round his mouth, just like the old man from Mogden Poo.

I walked over and picked up a box.
'FREE STICK-ON BEARD IN EVERY PACK!'
said a bright-red sticker, and I imagined
myself with a donut beard, looking
exactly like Class Captain.

on back
of pack

Mr Feeko's
**Beard
Flakes**

'Would you like to try one?' asked an old granny in a Feeko's uniform, and I did a blowoff out of shock, because I hadn't seen her sneak up.

She was wearing a name badge that said 'Pearl' and had a mole on the end of her nose that made her look like **Future Ratboy**'s mum.

Pearl held out a bowl of Beard Flakes and I picked one up and popped it on my tongue like it was a flattened-out bogie.

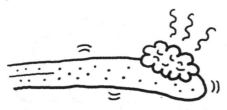

'EUUURRGGGHHHYYUCK!' I blurted, pretending to be sick all over Bunky, even though he wasn't there.

'Disgusting, aren't they!' chuckled Pearl. I looked at the price and the sticker saying 'FREE STICK-ON BEARD IN EVERY PACK!' and I smiled.

'I'll take thirty,' I said, reaching into my pocket for the coins, and Pearl did an old granny blowoff out of shock.

May the Keelest loser win

I felt a bit like an old granny myself, waddling through the school gates with my eight million Feeko's carrier bags filled with boxes of Beard Flakes.

Nancy was over by the table-tennis table, stacking the last three Whatever Boxes into a mini pyramid. 'Roll up, roll up, get your Whatever Boxes here!' she shouted as I walked towards her.

'Mornkeels,' I said, putting my bags down and lifting out a box of Beard Flakes. I opened the lid and poured the flakes into my rucksack and heard a really light thud, which was actually more like a thuh than a thud, not that I cared, because lying among the flakes was my free stick-on beard.

free stick-on
beard

'Er, what in the loserkeelness is going on here?' said Nancy, peering over my shoulder. 'Where did you get those?'

'Oh yeah, I borrowed some money off my mum,' I lied, sticking the beard on to my face. 'How do I look?'

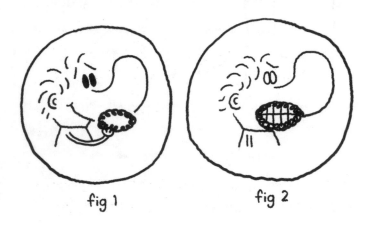

fig 1   fig 2

'Like a complete idiot,' said Nancy, doing one of her half-smiles. 'Have you got the ice cream tub, by the way?'

I put my hand in my pocket and felt the last coin left from all the money I'd stolen. It was that dirty, bent-in-half one Jocelyn Twiggs had bought his worm box with the other day.

'About that . . .' I said, trying to think of something to say. 'I've been sooo busy what with the election and everything, I COM-PER-LEE-TER-LY forgot to bring it,' I smiled, emptying more Beard Flakes into my rucksack and fishing around for the beards.

'Hmmm, well bring it in tomorrow,' said Nancy, doing a look like she didn't trust me at all times a million amen.

A poster saying 'ELECTION TOMORROW!' flew past my eyes and Sharonella and Fay appeared from behind it, as if by annoying magic.

'Good mornkeels, Barold,' said Sharonella. 'What's all this craziness, not that I even care . . .' she snorted, pointing at my beard.

'It's how I'm gonna win the election!'
I said, popping a stick-on beard back
into one of the emptied-out boxes. I
grabbed a pen from my pencil case
and crossed out 'Beard Flakes', writing
'Barry Loser' above it. 'A free Barry
Box for every vote!' I smiled, starting a
pyramid of my own.

feeling
really
keel

'Loserkeelness times a millikeels!' said
Fay in her perfect **Future Ratboy** voice,
and I fake smiled, pretending it didn't
make me really jealous.

Sharonella pulled a little pad out of her back pocket. 'IN-TER-RES-TER-ING,' she mumbled, jotting something down. 'May the keelest loser win, that's what I say!' she smiled, and then she waddled off, Fay following behind.

having an idea

The Donut Beards

'What's happenkeeling, loseroids!' said Bunky walking over, looking about a Fronkle taller. My eyes swivelled down and saw two cans of Fronkle strapped to his feet.

WOBBLE

Fronkle

I picked up a box and passed it to him. 'Vote for Barry!' I said, and he opened it up, pulling out a fake beard.

'It's like that old man's donut one at Mogden Poo!' laughed Bunky, sticking it on to his face, and we high fived like two old men with beards, one of them with Fronkle cans strapped to his feet.

me and Bunky when we're old

Nancy sighed, or it could have been the wind. 'Barry's mum was kind enough to buy him all these cereal boxes,' she said, kicking one of my carrier bags.

'Oh, and he forgot to bring in the ice cream tub . . . You know, the one with ALL OF OUR MONEY in it?'

I peeked at Nancy, who was doing that look I was talking about when she doesn't trust me at all times a million amen.

Then I looked at Bunky, who was standing there like a dog trying to work out what was going on between its two owners.

Bunky
dog

'Dazzoid!' I shouted, because Darren was walking past slurping on a Fronkle, plus I wanted to distract Bunky. 'Have a beard. One free with every vote!'

Darren wobbled over and picked up a box. 'Don't mind if I do!' he said, slapping it on to his mouth and taking another slurp. 'Mmm, Hairy Fronkle, how refreshypoos!' he burped, and Nancy covered her nose.

I smiled to myself, thinking how well my idea was working out. Then I remembered the empty ice cream tub underneath my bed, and stopped smiling.

'How could you steal from your best friends?' whispered a mini Barry from his brain sofa, and I shook my head to myself, feeling like a naughty little Superloser.

my skull

watching my life like a movie

'Nancy, what about you?' said Bunky, waggling his beard and passing her a box. 'Vote for Barry?'

'I'm still deciding,' said Nancy, giving me her look again, and I hoped she couldn't hear my mini Barry.

The White-boards

When the bell went I took down my pyramid of boxes and headed into class, smiling in the middle of my donut beard because our first lesson was Art, which is one of my COM-PER-LEET and utter favourites.

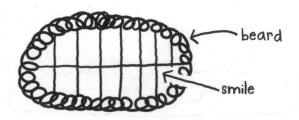

beard

smile

As soon as I walked through the door I spotted Sharonella and Fay sitting in the corner with a big pile of white cardboard, both of them holding scissors.

'What's all this unloserkeelness?' I said, walking the long way round to my desk so I could have a look.

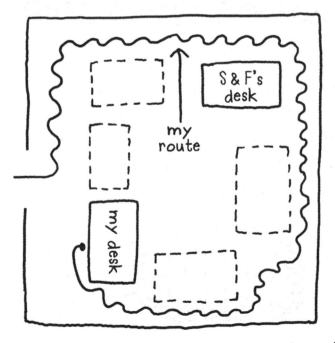

'You'll see!' snortled Sharonella, cutting a rectangle of cardboard and making two holes at the top. She snipped a bit of string off a bundle on the floor and threaded it through the holes.

looks familiar

I sat down at my desk and thought about what to draw. Outside the wind was blowing, and I Superloser-zoomed my eyes in, trying to work out what wind actually looks like. And that's when I heard Sharonella's voice.

'ROLL UP, ROLL UP, get your whiteboards over here!' she shouted, holding one of the cardboard rectangles above her head. 'Free whiteboard with every vote for Fay!'

I couldn't believe my ears, which by the way had just gone COM-PER-LEET-ER-LY red out of annoyance. Sharonella and Fay had TOTALLY copied my idea.

my
ear

me not
believing it

'Shush, Sharonella!' shushed Miss Spivak, and Honk flew off her shoulder and out the door because he's scared of the 'sh' sound, which must be pretty difficult for Miss Spivak seeing as she's got a really loud and annoying Sharonella in her class. 'Honkypoos! Come to Mama!' she warbled, running out the door after him.

Jocelyn's chair screeched out from under his desk and he ran round to Sharonella. 'Ooh, me! Me!' he squeaked, picking a whiteboard up and putting it round his neck.

Sharonella grabbed a pencil and wrote 'VOTE FOR FAY!' in massive capitals, right across the board.

My ears went even redder and I
imagined my mini Barrys sweating
on their brain sofa.

'That's COM-PER-LEET-ER-LY copying
my loserkeelness!' I screamed, my
donut beard half falling off.

not getting
TOO annoyed

'She did the same thing with our dog drawings,' moaned Donnatella, holding up her sheet, which was full of drawings of dogs, and Tracy nodded, holding hers up too.

'Stuart!' I shouted, and Stuart Shmendrix jumped. 'Put this donut beard on immedikeely!' I said, fishing one out of a box and throwing it over Nancy's head.

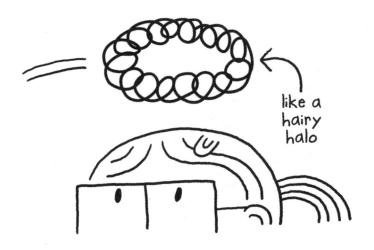

like a hairy halo

Nancy turned round and looked up at me, the way my mum does when I'm being naughty. I looked at her piece of paper and saw a drawing of the Feeko's ice cream tub, with me dressed as a burglar standing next to it.

Stuart took the beard and held it up to his face, not sure if he wanted to put it on or not.

'Darren!' I shouted, and Darren reached across and squodged the beard on to Stuart's lips. 'WE ARE THE DONUT BEARDS!' I boomed, and Bunky stood up to do a salute and fell over straight away, probably because of his stupid Fronkle feet.

slightly angry

'Barry Loser, will you sit down NOW!' screamed Miss Spivak, coming back in with Honk on her shoulder.

I sat back down, picked my pencil up and started to draw the wind, my hands shaking.

I tried to think of something nice that would calm me down a bit, and remembered it was my birthday coming up.

last year's cake
(only one R in pack)

I smiled to myself and thought of the **Future Ratboy** trainers I'd asked my mum and dad for, and felt my radiator ears start to cool down.

'Psst! Sharonella!' whispered Anton, who was sitting next to her and Fay. 'Can I have a couple?' he said, and Sharonella passed two whiteboards down to him and Gaspar, and another one for Anton's invisible friend, Invis, not that he hangs out with him much any more.

I pressed my pencil down and the point snapped from how shaky my hand was. It flew across the desk and landed on Nancy's drawing of me as a burglar, making a little 'V' shape above my eyes, like I had evil eyebrows.

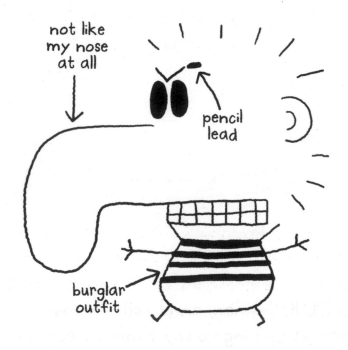

not like my nose at all

pencil lead

burglar outfit

'Can you believe Sharonella!' I whispered to Nancy, my voice all wobbling like the voice of a jelly, if jellies could talk, which they so can't.

my
voice

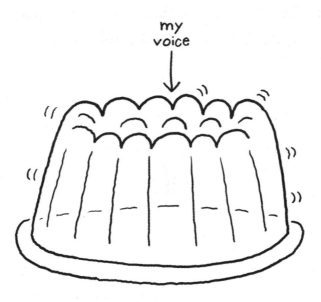

'Hmmm,' hmmmed Nancy, doing a brand new look I'd never seen before, where she doesn't trust me at all times a ZILLION amen, and I felt my mini Barrys turning up my radiator ears.

Lord Donut

After that it was lunch. While my main Donut Beard followers Darren, Stuart and Bunky gave out a few more donut beards, I watched Sharonella and Fay going round the playground hanging whiteboards round people's necks.

Then the bell went and we all got into the coach and headed off on a trip to the recycling centre.

'Grubbage was supposed to meet us here,' said Miss Spivak after we'd parked and got off the bus in the corner of Feeko's car park, 'but he called this morning and said he had a particularly bad case of Zeditis, whatever that is . . .'

I snortled to myself, because Zeditis is this made-up disease I pretend to have whenever I want to get out of something.

been snoring Zs all night

stuck under them

'Ohhhhh,' groaned everyone, because we all wanted to see Grubbage again, but maybe not smell him. Then we trudged over to the huge green metal recycling bins with the holes in their sides.

'Barry, take this stuff,' said Miss Spivak, passing me a massive box full of plastic bottles, and I wished I had Fronkle cans strapped to my feet so I could reach the holes.

'Darren, you're in charge of glass. Now who can I give the paper to . . . Ah yes, Fay and Sharonella!' shouted Miss Spivak, and Honk flew off her shoulder, probably because of the 'sh' sound.

I glanced over at Sharonella and Fay and all their loserish followers stuffing sheets of paper into the bins, and I imagined myself posting all their stupid whiteboards in there too.

Darren had lined up ten green bottles and was standing in front of a bin, throwing them at the holes.

SMASH! broke the first one, hitting the side and exploding into a million bits. A shard of glass whooshed past Nancy's face, and she gave me one of her looks, even though it wasn't ME who'd done it, it was Darren, like I just said.

'Darren Darrenofski!' screeched Miss
Spivak, or it could have been Honk,
who was pecking around on the
floor for crumbs. 'Stop that NOW!'

Darren turned to me and smiled inside
his beard. 'What do I do, boss?' he said,
holding up another bottle.

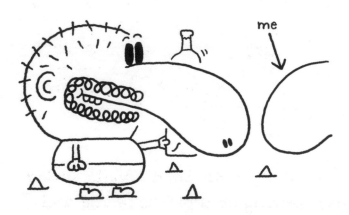

me

'Yeah Barry, can we throw them or what?' giggled Stuart, and a few more Donut Beards walked over too.

'Tell us what to do, Lord Donut!' smiled Bunky, picking up a plastic bottle and aiming it at a hole.

Nancy appeared next to me with her
last Whatever Box under her arm.
'Tell them to stop it, Barry,' she said.
'That last one almost hit me.'

'Helpypoos, that last one awmowst
hit me,' baby-voiced Stuart Shmendrix,
wobbling up and grabbing the Whatever
Box out from under Nancy's arm.

He ran over to the cardboard bin and held it up to the hole. 'Shall I put it in?' he laughed, his donut beard hanging off his face.

'Give it back, Stuart!' screamed Nancy, running after him, and he waggled the box up in the air.

'Tell us what to do, Lord Donut!' shouted the Donut Beards all together, and I scratched my bum, wondering what I should say.

'You have to give your voters what they WANT!' whispered a mini Barry in my head, and the wind blew, ruffling the hairs in my beard.

'DO IT,' I said, turning round so I didn't have to see.

After that last bit

'It's only a cardboard box, you can have one of my spare ones!' I said, tapping Nancy on the shoulder as we arrived back at school, but she just shrugged and walked off. 'OK, I'll see you tomorrow then. Don't forget it's my birthday next week!' I shouted, and she disappeared round the corner, leaving me with all the Donut Beards.

'What now, Lord Donut?' said Darren, everyone standing behind him waiting for me to give them their next order.

'Get a good night's sleep,' I said, all Class-Captainly. 'And remember to vote for me tomorrow!'

The Donut Beards walked off and me and Bunky headed home, him wobbling along on his Fronkle feet. 'So, what have you got me for my birthday?' I said, because we always get each other birthday presents.

Bunky opened his mouth as if he was about to say something, then changed his mind and shut it, then opened it again.

OPEN

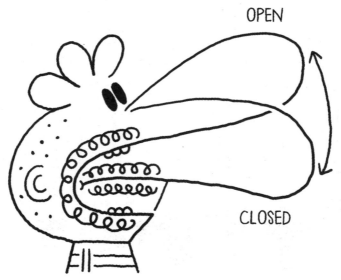

CLOSED

'Oh . . . right, so it's your birthday is it?' he said, all weirdly. 'I completely and utterly forgot about that. Honest I did. Errrrmmmm . . . are you gonna have a party?'

Lord Donut

'Yeeeeessssss,' I said, which is how **Future Ratboy** says 'yes' when he thinks someone's up to something but can't be bothered to find out what's going on.

We talked about my birthday party until we got to the top of my road, which is where I go my way and he goes his.

Some Street

Walnut Tree Close

FEEKO'S

'Biggest day in the history of days ever tomozzoid!' I said, giving him a salute, and he quadruple-twizzle-saluted me back.

'See you tomozzoid, Lord Donut!' shouted Bunky. 'Oh. Yes. Erm. And don't forget the ice cream tub!'

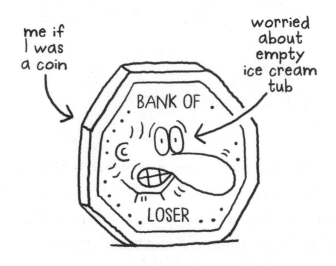

me if I was a coin

worried about empty ice cream tub

BANK OF

LOSER

Tomozzoid

Before you could say 'tomorrow' it was the next day and I was walking back to the top of my road, this time from the other direction.

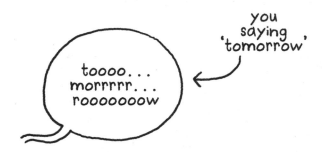

'Mornkeels!' said Bunky, still with the Fronkle cans on his feet. He stuck his donut beard on and I gave him a little salute. 'Erm, where's that ice cream tub I was talking about?'

'Oh yeah, about that . . .' I said, trying to think of a lie. 'You would not BEEE-LIEEEEVE how busy I've been, what with the election and everything . . . you know, I COM-PER-LEET-ER-LY forgot to bring it,' I smiled, heading off for school.

'That's OK, just erm . . . just go back and get it!' said Bunky all weirdly, pointing at my house, which was about three metres away.

'I would LOVE to, Bunkypoos, really I would, but I just HAAAVE to get to school,' I said, and I carried on walking, hoping that was that.

'But . . .' said Bunky, and I turned round to face him.

'LORD DONUT SAYS NO!' I screamed, and Bunky jumped, falling off his Fronkle cans. I helped him up and we walked to school, not saying much at all amen.

The loserkeelest superloser

The Donut Beards were waiting for me at the school gates when we got there, chanting 'Loser!' over and over again, which is a weird thing to hear when what you really want is to be the winner.

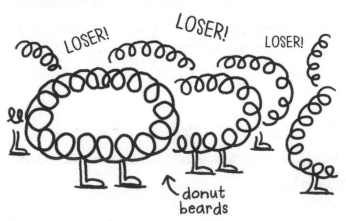

LOSER! LOSER! LOSER!

← donut beards

'Good luck, Barry,' said the Future-Ratboyest voice ever, and I turned round and saw Fay standing there, reaching out her hand.

'May the loserkeelest superloser win!' I said, shaking hands, and Gaspar took a photo.

'Vote time!' screeched Honk over the loudspeaker, and we all ran into the classroom and started queuing up by the big board, which still stank a bit of bins, thank* to Grubbage from the other day.

* smallest thank ever

The vote

Voting was the easiest thing ever amen. All you had to do was go behind the board and write who you were voting for on a piece of paper and slot it into a little box, and that was it.

so the pencil can't escape

I tried to count how many Donut Beards there were compared to Whiteboards, but I kept getting confused because of everyone walking around, so in the end I gave up and sat down, crossing all my fingers and toes.

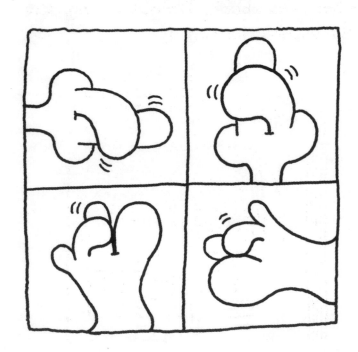

'That's everyone,' said Miss Spivak once we'd all voted apart from Nancy. 'Apart from Nancy Verkenwerken.'

I looked around the classroom and spotted Nancy at the back, working on a new design for Whatever Boxes in her sketchbook. 'I'm not voting,' she said, without looking up.

'Come on, Nancy!' I smiled,
pretending I'd forgotten about her
being in a mood with me, but she just
carried on scribbling.

'In that case it's lunchtime,' said Miss
Spivak, and we all ran out into the
playground, apart from Nancy.

The
end

(Only joking.)

Lunch breath

I can't remember what I had for my packed lunch, but before I knew it I was back in the classroom sitting in my seat, with my breath smelling of cheese-and-pickle sandwiches, a tangerine, two Feeko's chocolate digestives and a can of Caffeine Free Diet Cherry Fronkle.

'I have some very interesting news, kiddywinkles!' said Miss Spivak, holding a sheet of paper in her hands. 'Honk and I counted the votes up over lunch, and it seems we have a TIE!'

I glanced over at Fay, wondering if we should have been best friends instead of enemies, seeing as we're EX-ACK-ER-LY as loserkeel as each other.

Then I thought how she'd COM-PER-LEET-ER-LY copied my loserkeelness, and I went back to thinking she was the most annoying loseroid ever.

me thinking
we could
be friends

me thinking
she's really
annoying

'OMG, Miss, we should SERIOUSLY flip a coin!' cried Sharonella, standing up.

'Good idea Sharonella, does anyone have a coin?' said Miss Spivak, Honk flying off her shoulder, and I remembered I still had one left over from when I bought my Beard Flakes.

'I've got one!' I said, putting my hand in my pocket and pulling out the dirtiest, bent-in-halfest coin ever. 'Heads!' I called, flipping it into the air.

And that's when it happened.

The winner

'That coin . . . It looks familiar,' murmured Nancy from the back of the classroom. The coin paused in mid-air like **Future Ratboy** at the end of one of his episodes, except more coin-like. 'Where did you get that?' said Nancy, walking over and standing right in front of me.

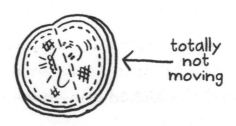

totally not moving

She stuck her hand out and the coin
landed in her palm.

The Feeko's carrier bags with my
leftover Barry Boxes were under my
desk, and she kicked one, making it
rustle.

'Your mum didn't lend you any money, did she?' said Nancy. 'This is Jocelyn's coin. I remember him buying a Whatever Box with it. I put it in the ice cream tub with all the other coins. Then you STOLE THEM and bought those Beard Flakes, DIDN'T YOU!' she said, all in one go.

acting all innocent

Outside, the wind had stopped.
I waited for a mini Barry to whisper something in my ear, but nothing happened.

I looked over at Bunky, hoping he wouldn't believe it. His face was like a dog's when its owner's being horrible.

WHIMPER

'How could you, Barry?' he shouted, ripping off his donut beard and throwing it at my feet. 'We were saving up to buy you a **Future Ratboy** costume with it too!'

I remembered Bunky being all weird about my birthday, and Nancy when she said she was saving up for a sun lounger.

'But . . .' I mumbled, but there was nothing left to say.

Miss Spivak came over and peered into Nancy's hand. 'Heads it is. Congratulations Barry, looks like you're the winner,' she smiled.

The word 'winner' floated into my earhole and echoed round my brain, and I thought back to how this all started, with me thinking I was such a superloser.

'I'm sorry, Nancy. I'm sorry, Bunky,'
I whispered, looking down at the floor.

'You're not sorry for anything,' said
Nancy, dropping the coin on to Bunky's
donut beard and walking away.
'You got exactly what you wanted,
Barry WINNER.'

Barry
Winner

Lip wobble

It was lonely walking home all on my own with no Bunky or Nancy to talk to, and no mini Barrys sitting on their brain sofa telling me what to do.

I even missed the wind, which had stopped blowing, and I felt my bottom lip start to wobble as I trudged down my road.

what
no wind ⟶
looks like
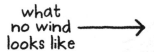

'What's wrong with my little Snookyflumps?' warbled my mum as she opened the front door, and I fell into her, like a pyramid of Barry Boxes collapsing in the no-wind.

Onion tears

'Barry Garry Larry Loser, what DID get into you?' said my mum after I'd told her everything, and I knew I'd been bad, because she only uses my middle names when I'm a VERY naughty Barrypoos.

'I'm sowwy, Mumsy,' I said in my Baby Barry voice, and my mum pretended to be sick all over Bunky, even though he wasn't there, because he hates me.

'It's Nancy and Bunky you need to apologise to,' she said, chopping up an onion and crying from the fumes, and I leaned over to get some of them into my eyes.

I imagined my mini Barrys turning little taps on behind my eyeballs, then remembered they were gone.

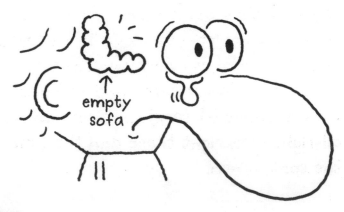

empty sofa

'I don't think Nancy and Bunky like me any more,' I cried, leaning against my mum's leg, and she stroked my hair like I was her pet cat.

PURRRRRR

'What if they don't want to come to my birthday as well?' I bawled, and I imagined my party without Bunky and Nancy there and came up with a kind-of-loserish-but-sort-of-all-right plan right there and then on the spot, amen.

Grubbarry

My kind-of-loserish-but-sort-of-all-right plan was this:

1. Cancel my birthday party as a tell-off to myself for being such a naughty Barrypoos

2. Go into school and tell everyone, looking all sad

3. Wait for Nancy and Bunky to feel really sorry for me

4. Let them forgive me for stealing all their money

5. Go back to my normal loserkeel life

I was so excited I didn't even brush my teeth on Monday morning, so my breath smelt like Grubbage as I skateboarded to school all alone.

totally dry

FUTURE
RATBOY

KIDS

My no-donut-beard non-waggled in the no-wind, and I smiled to myself, imagining Nancy and Bunky being my best friends again.

'Here he comes! Captain Loser!' burped
Darren Darrenofski in his donut beard
as I walked into the classroom.

'Please, Loserfans, don't stand up,'
I said, keeping him and all the other
Donut Beards happy, even though
donut beards are COM-PER-LEET-ER-LY
over.

standing up
anyway

Nancy and Bunky were sitting in their seats, staring out of the window at the no-wind, not that you can see something that isn't even there.

'Mornkeels,' I said, sitting down next to them, but they just ignored me. 'Did you hear the news?'

Nancy opened her sketchbook and started drawing a Whatever Box, and Bunky pretended he was thinking about something, even though I know for a FACT he never thinks about ANYTHING.

inside Bunky's head

'My birthday party's been cancelled because of how much of a naughty Barry I was,' I said, doing my extra-sad face, where my nose droops down.

that face I was just talking about

I stuck my bottom lip out and made it wobble, waiting for them to feel sorry for me and forgive me.

'Your breath stinks like Grubbage,'
said Nancy, doing her face she does
when she doesn't like me at all times
a million amen.

Grubbage
breath

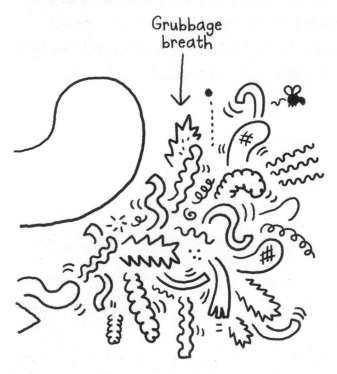

I shut my mouth and sat there feeling
like a comperleet loser.

'Yeah Grubbarry, I can totally smell your breath from over here!' snortled Sharonella, and everyone laughed apart from me, because it's really hard to laugh when your bottom lip is actually real-life wobbling.

Verbunken-notloser

I spent the rest of the morning doing my lessons all normally, apart from the fact I didn't have my best friends to talk to.

just fancy a little chat

'Captain Loser, there's a meeting at lunchtime for teachers and all Class Captains regarding the layout of the new car park. It shouldn't take more than an hour,' said Miss Spivak halfway through Maths, which is definitely the most boring sentence ever said.

Miss Spivak's car

I thought about sighing, then changed my mind and did a blowoff instead, wishing I'd never started this whole Class Captain thing in the first place, seeing as it'd COM-PER-LEET-ER-LY ruined my life.

Then it was lunchtime and I trudged up the stairs to the staffroom with Miss Spivak, talking about how well the new brooms have been working, because that's what you do when you're Class Captain.

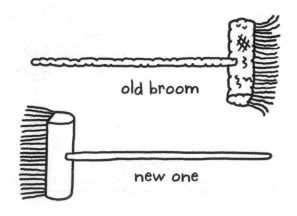

old broom

new one

'How are you enjoying the job, Captain Loser?' asked Mr Koops after we'd talked about the car park for about nine hours, and I fake smiled, glancing out of the window at all the other kids running around in the playground being happy.

Hanging on the brick wall behind the table-tennis table was a big poster with the words Verbunkenloser Ltd written on it, except the 'loser' bit had been rubbed off, a bit like the 'L' in Mogden Poo.

don't know who this is →

I zoomed my eyes in and saw Nancy and Bunky standing round the table, selling their new-design Whatever Boxes.

My kind-of-loserish-but-sort-of-all-right plan had failed, and now I was all alone for the rest of my life, amen.

me in
fifty
years

'Don't be so unkeel, Superloser! You just have to come up with one of your BRILLIANT and AMAZEKEEL plans!' said a voice inside my head, and I didn't know if it was a mini Barry or just me thinking it, but either way I'd had enough of my stupid plans.

'This is a job for Barry Loser,' I whispered to myself, and Mr Koops looked at me like I was going mad.

Happy birthkeel

'Happy birthday, Snookyflumps!' said my mum two mornings later as I left for school, and she handed me a little box of Feeko's Raisins for my present. 'I'm so proud of you!' she called out, and I popped a couple of raisins into my mouth for good luck.

NOT
Nostril
Raisins

Feeko's
Raisins

'Happy birthkeel to you . . .' I heard as I skateboarded up to the school gates ten minutes later, and I felt my heart start to beat.

I was sure no one had remembered it was my birthday today, what with them all hating me and everything.

Then I turned round the corner and saw Fay being given the bumps. Everyone was standing around her, singing the Happy Birthday tune, and I rolled my eyes and did a little snortle.

'Typikeel. You and Fay have exackerly the same birthday!' laughed a mini Barry, or maybe it was just me thinking it.

'HAPPY BIRTHKEEL FAY,' I said, going up to her after the bumps had finished. Not that I actually said it out loud.

What with all the talking I'd been doing in my Class Captain meetings, I'd got a sore throat, so I'd scribbled it on to the white plastic board thingy that was hanging round my neck.

HAPPY
BIRTHKEEL
FAY

looks familiar

'Hey, that's the sort of loserkeel thing I'd do!' she said, and I reached into my rucksack and pulled out a cardboard box.

'HAVE A BEARD FLAKE,' I wrote on my board, and she stuck her hand in and put a flake on to her tongue.

'EUUURRGGGHHHYYUCK!!!' she screamed, spitting it out all over Bunky, who'd appeared next to her with Nancy. 'Actually, they're not bad!' she laughed, and I gave her the whole pack.

donut beard Fay

I reached into my rucksack again and pulled out a big wrapping-papered box with red ribbon round it.

'THIS IS FOR YOU TWO,' I wrote, handing over the box, and Nancy took it without smiling.

Everything paused, like at the end of a **Future Ratboy** episode. I couldn't hear a thing, not even the wind.

Loser boy

'Maybe you should open it?' said Fay in her **Future Ratboy** voice, and I popped a raisin into my mouth, waiting to see what they'd do.

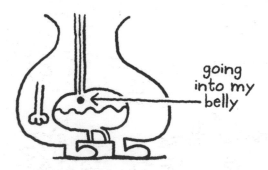

going into my belly

'Only because it's your birthday,' said
Nancy, and Bunky grabbed the present
and ripped off the paper.

'Our empty Feeko's ice cream tub,' he
said, his nose drooping. 'The one you
stole all the money out of.'

disappointed
nose

pointed
nose

ICE CREAM

'TA-DA . . .' I wrote on my whiteboard in ginormous letters, and I lifted the lid off the box.

Inside were four notes, enough to buy a pair of **Future Ratboy** trainers for my birthday present, except I'd told my mum to put the money in the ice cream box for me to give back to Nancy and Bunky instead.

'Our money!' said Bunky, pulling out a big green note.

'Captain Loser, you're late for your meeting,' shouted Miss Spivak across the playground, and I started to walk towards the staffroom.

'Barry,' I heard, and I hoped it wasn't a mini Barry whispering in my head.

'Yeah?' I said in my head, because I couldn't speak thanks to my sore throat, and I turned round, crossing all my fingers and toes, which is hard to do when you're in the middle of turning round.

'Happy birthkeel!' cried Nancy and Bunky, and Fay too. They handed me a yellow Whatever Box, which is the new colour for Whatever Boxes these days in case you didn't know.

wonder what's inside?

NEW!

WHAT EVER!

Now with even more whatever!

'FOR ME?' I scribbled, taking the box, and a crowd started to gather around, including Sharonella, Donnatella and Tracy, who I think might have made friends and started drawing cats instead, seeing as they all had biro-cat-tattoos on their bracelet arms.

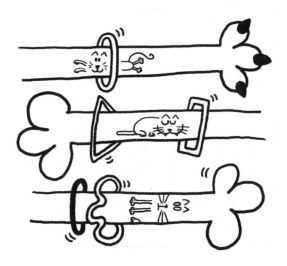

'OPEN IT!' squawked Honk, who was sitting on Miss Spivak's shoulder as per usual.

I slid my finger along the top of the box and flipped the lid, putting my hand inside, and lifted out the smelliest-looking, most-faded-ever plastic 'L' I'd seen in my entire life on this planet amen.

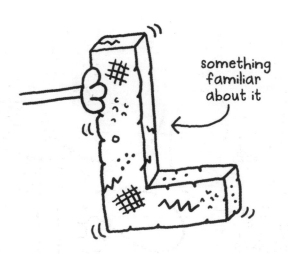

something familiar about it

'I found it down a drain near Mogden Poo!' said Bunky, and I looked at the 'L' and realised what it was . . . The one from the Mogden Poo sign that'd disappeared eight million years ago!

'KEELNESS!' I scribbled on my whiteboard, and I held the 'L' in front of my chest, exackerly where **Future Ratboy** has his 'R', and cleared my sore throat.

bit bigger than **Future** Ratboy's 'R'

'Loserboy to the rescue!' I squeaked, jumping in the air like **Future Ratboy** at the end of his TV show, and Honk flew off Miss Spivak's shoulder and did a poo right on Fay's goldfish hair clip, which is probably the loserkeelest thing that has ever happened in the history of the universe amen.

And for some reason I COM-PER-LEE-TER-LY didn't care.

Not the end

(Is really.)

About the
page numberer

Jim Smith is the keelest kids' book page numberer in the whole wide world amen.

He graduated from art school with first class honours (the best you can get) and went on to create the branding for a sweet little chain of coffee shops.

He also designs cards and gifts under the name Waldo Pancake.

'Page numbering is my real passion,' says Jim, numbering a page and chuckling to himself. 'There's nothing I hate more than a page that isn't numbered.'